THE MERMAID TALES

CELIA'S BEST FRIENDS

CHLOE SANDERS

The Mermaid Tales

Celia's Best Friends

by Chloe Sanders

The water was warm. The bright yellow sun crossed over the white sand on the beaches of Lilysong. The island breezes sang through the palm trees and made music that Celia could dance to.

Yes, mermaids dance. They dance in the water. Celia splashed and spun in circles and dove deep under the water before launching herself up, up, up! She reached for the sky, but it was too far for her to touch.

That was fine with Celia. She splashed back down into the water and dove deep, deep, deeper into the ocean. Her long, silvery hair curled around her and her pale blue scales sparkled and shimmered on her mermaid tail. She wore her favorite shells today. They matched her shiny tail. Everyone thought she looked like a princess with her necklace of shiny pink stones. Today was a day for having fun, and Celia laughed and sang as she went looking for her friend Billy.

Of course, mermaids can sing and laugh and even talk under the water. Everyone knows that. Did you know they can also talk to the fish? All the other sea animals, too. Celia reached the bottom of the ocean around Lilysong, where the purple and green and orange coral created patterns of color like a crazy, beautiful painting. The sea was so full of pretty things. Celia was happy she got to live here in the City of Pearl. That was where her home was. That was where her mother and father and little sister Trixie lived. It was the best place in the whole, big world.

For a while Celia had fun playing tag with an octopus named Ophelia. The two friends laughed and swam around each other in a stone garden. Ophelia won most of the games. After all, she had eight arms!

There were a lot of friends in the ocean. Celia always had someone to play with. She had fun with Ophelia, but she really wanted to find Billy. They were supposed to go exploring today. So she said goodbye to Ophelia and swam off, hoping to find Billy at the Tall Stones.

Not far from the City of Pearl there were stones that stood taller than giants, rising up out of the water. Gray stones that were all different shapes. Some of them looked like giant men. Some of them looked like big fish, leaping out of the ocean. Others didn't look like anything at all. They made a maze that was so fun to swim through. It was a great place to play hide and seek.

Even before she got to the Tall Stones, Celia heard Billy laughing.

Chee-ree-ree, Billy laughed. He liked to laugh, and have fun, and he was great at a lot of games. Celia and Billy spent hours together every day, exploring and playing with their friends.

Billy was a blue dolphin. He was almost as good at swimming as Celia, even if he couldn't stay underwater for very long. He loved a good joke, and he loved to have fun, and he and Celia were the best of friends.

In the shadow of a giant tower of stone that looked like a huge ice cream cone, Billy laughed and swam backward on his tail when he saw Celia. "Hi!" he shouted. "Are you ready to have fun?"

"You know it!" Celia said. Then she dove underneath Billy in the water, and when she came back up she tagged Billy on his chin. "You're it!"

The two friends swam through the Tall Stones chasing each other, laughing, and finding secret tunnels through the big rocks. "I like being your friend," Billy told Celia. "You're always fun."

"We always have fun together," Celia told Billy, because she knew what it meant to be a good friend. Celia was friends with everyone because she was nice, and she was fun, and everyone in the City of Pearl liked her.

"Want to have a race?" Billy challenged Celia. "From here to the big rock that looks like a tree. Ready, set, go!"

Billy swam as fast as he could. Billy was fast, but Celia was faster. She swished her tail and swam, swam, swam!

Before they got to the turtle shaped rock, Celia stopped. She saw something. Not just something. Someone.

Celia saw one of the animals in the sea who didn't know how to be a good friend.

Squatina the Shark was swimming circles around a much smaller fish. She was a white shark with big black eyes and rows of sharp teeth. She was always being mean to fish and animals that were smaller than her.

Billy stopped the race, too. He swam next to Celia and watched Squatina the Shark tease and bully a little orange and white clownfish. The smaller fish was so scared he kept spinning in little circles, spin spinspin, spin spinspin. Squatina was calling the poor clownfish mean names, and wouldn't let him go anywhere.

"Come on," Billy said. "Let's go swim somewhere else. It won't be any fun with Squatina here."

Celia wanted to have fun today,
but she couldn't just leave. Not
when there was someone in trouble.
"We can have fun later," she told
Billy. "Right now that little fish

needs our help. We need to be good friends and help everyone we can."

Billy smiled at Celia. "You're right. I'm just a little scared. Squatina is big, and mean. She's a shark!"

"Even sharks want to have friends," Celia promised. "Come on, let's go see if we can help."

Billy wasn't sure he wanted to go over to where Squatina swam her circles around the little fish, but he followed Celia, and soon they were face to face with the big white shark. She was even scarier up close.

Celia smiled at the shark, and at the little stripy fish, who was all blown up like a balloon because he was so scared.

Squatina hadn't stopped swimming. She wasn't doing circles around the clownfish anymore, but she was still swimming, back and forth, back and forth.

Now she watched Celia and Billy with a big, black eye. "What do you two want?" Squatina asked in a cold, shaky voice.

"We wanted to come meet the best swimmer in the ocean," Celia told Squatina.

Squatina was confused. "Who, me?" she asked.

"Of course," Celia said. "You must be a great swimmer. Mermaids are good swimmers, sure, but I'll bet sharks are even better."

The shark smiled a big, toothy grin. "I am a good swimmer. I'm better than you, Celia."

"Oh, I don't know about that," Billy said, with a little dolphin laugh. "My friend Celia is the best swimmer I know."

"I'm better!" Squatina shouted. "I'm the best swimmer in the whole wide ocean!"

"Really?" Billy asked.

"Really," Squatina said, "and I can prove it! I'll race both of you. Ready, set, go!"

Squatina took off through the Tall Stones, swimming as fast as Celia had ever seen a shark swim.

Celia looked at Billy. Billy looked at Celia. They had tricked the shark.

Now she was swimming away, instead of being mean.

The little orange and white clownfish watched the shark swim away. He looked at the shark, and then he looked at Celia, and then he smiled a slow, slow smile. He wasn't scared anymore, now that Squatina was gone. "Aren't you guys going to race with her?" he asked.

"No," Celia said. "I don't need to prove who the fastest swimmer is. I don't need to be better than her. I just need to be a good friend. We saw how Squatina was treating you. We wanted to help."

"Thank you," said the clownfish. "I was so scared. That shark was so big!"

Celia swam over and gave the clownfish a big hug. "Trouble always looks too big when we try to take care of it by ourselves. When we have good friends to help us, that always makes trouble look smaller. Look at the shark now."

The clownfish looked where Celia pointed. Sure enough, the

further away Squatina swam, the smaller she looked.

Chee-ree-ree,Billy laughed, dancing around on his tail in a big circle. "Let's play! Let's play!"

Celia thought that was a great idea. "Do you want to come with us?" Celia asked the clownfish. "My friend and I were going to explore all day, and play games, and have a picnic lunch. We always have room for one more friend."

"That sounds great!" the clownfish said. "I'm so glad that I met you guys. My name is Alex."

"We're glad we met you, too," Celia told him. "My name is Celia, and this is Billy the dolphin. Come on, let's go swim over to Lilysong Island. The wind is making wonderful music there today!"

The three friends all agreed that sounded like a great idea, but before they could leave, Squatina the shark came swimming back over.

"Hey," Squatina said, her voice a little sad. "You guys didn't race with me."

"No," Billy said. "We didn't. You were being mean to our friend Alex."

Squatina looked confused. "Who's Alex?"

Alex puffed out his chest a little bit. "I am," he said. "You were being mean to me."

"Oh," Squatina said. "Was I? I thought I was just having fun."

"I didn't think it was fun," Alex said. "You said mean things to me, and you wouldn't let me leave when I wanted to."

Squatina swam back and forth, back and forth. "But that's just how I am," she said. "I'm a shark. No one ever wants to play with a shark, so I have to make them play with me."

"Well," Billy said, "it wasn't very nice."

Celia swished the tip of her blue tail as she swam a little closer to Squatina the shark. "Not everyone in the ocean knows how to be a good friend. If you want people to be your friends, then you have to be a friend to them."

Squatina flashed her big, sharp teeth. "But it's fun to make other animals be afraid."

"No, it isn't!" Alex said, swimming over to hide behind Billy's fin.

"Oh," Squatina said, "I think it is." Alex yelped and spun in his little circles.

"Well," Celia said, turning away from the shark, "my friends and I are going to go dance and sing at Lilysong Island. If you just want to make people scared and mad, then you will have to stay here by yourself. If you want to come with us, then you will have to be nicer."

Squatina blinked her big, black eyes. "You really want me to come with you?"

"If you want to," Celia said. "But only if you can be nice to us and to our new friend."

The big white shark sank a little lower in the water. "I'm not sure I know how to be nice," she said. "All I've ever been is a shark. I don't know how to be anything else."

"Just because you're a shark," Celia said, "doesn't mean you can't be nice. Why don't you come with us, and we can help you learn to be a good friend.

Squatina took a big, deep breath of ocean water. "I would like that. I've never had a real friend before." "Then you can start with us," Celia said. "If you promise not to be mean anymore, and if you really try, then we can be your friends, and you can be ours."

Squatina promised, and the four of them swam all the way to Lilysong Island together. The wind blew through the trees and made a song that was better than any song Celia had ever heard there before. The sun was warm, and the water was wet, and even the pink flamingos that flew over the island were happy and playful.

They spent the rest of the day there, and Celia and Billy and Alex showed Squatina how to play games without cheating. They showed her how to say nice things instead of calling names and teasing. They even showed her how to wait her turn and let others have a try.

By the end of the day, when the sun was setting, Squatina had learned how to make new friends.

Squatina swam up close to Alex the clownfish, and she whispered, "I'm sorry I was mean to you. Now I know what it means to be a real friend. Will you be my friend?"Alex smiled, and whispered back, "I would like that, very much."

Celia said goodbye to her new friends as the bright orange ball of the sun touched the water and began to sink out of sight. Then she gave Billy a big hug. "I had a lot of fun today," she told Billy. "Will you be here tomorrow?""Of course I will," Billy told her. "A day in the ocean is always more fun with you." "Friends forever?" Celia asked. "Forever friends," Billy promised.

And the two of them swam home, to wait for more fun and adventure tomorrow.

—the end—

Made in the USA
Middletown, DE
17 December 2016